13.96   9-4-08   3146990E

This book
belongs to

For Marije

FREDERICK WARNE

Published by the Penguin Group
Penguin Books Ltd, 80 Strand, London WC2R 0RL, England
Penguin Young Readers Group, 345 Hudson Street,
New York, New York 10014, U.S.A.
Penguin Books Australia Ltd, 250 Camberwell Road, Camberwell,
Victoria 3124, Australia
Canada, India, New Zealand, South Africa

1

ISBN-13: 978 07232 59046

Printed in Great Britain

Candytuft's Enchanting Treats

by Kay Woodward

Welcome to the Flower Fairies Garden!

Where are the fairies?
Where can we find them?
We've seen the fairy-rings
They leave behind them!

Is it a secret
No one is telling?
Why, in your garden
Surely they're dwelling!

No need for journeying,
Seeking afar:
Where there are flowers,
There fairies are!

Contents

Chapter One
Fairy Friendship Week   1

Chapter Two
Try and Try Again   17

Chapter Three
Meddlesome Mischief   33

Chapter Four
More Strange Happenings   45

Chapter Five
Mysterious Visitors   55

Chapter Six
Sweet Victory   65

Fairy Friendship Week

"You're totally sure?" Candytuft said earnestly. "I mean, it would be completely wonderful if you did, but I wouldn't want you to go to any trouble—"

"I really think you ought to take a breath now," said Lavender with a giggle. "Honestly, it would be my pleasure. It is Fairy Friendship Week, after all."

Of course! A wonderfully warm feeling rushed from Candytuft's dainty toes to the tips of her pearly pink wings and back again. Of all the festivals and parties held each year in Flower Fairyland—and there were quite a lot of these, because fairies just *love* special occasions—this had to be her absolute favorite.

Fairy Friendship Week was a time for fairies to spoil each other silly, with treats and surprises galore. If Flower Fairies could

think of an extra-special way to cheer up a friend, they would. If they could help out with the dullest tasks to brighten a fairy's day, they'd do that too. And this was precisely why Lavender had offered to do Candytuft's laundry.

"This is ever so kind of you," said Candytuft, scrambling frantically below the white, pink and purple blossoms of her flower. "However hard I scrub my clothes, they never look as spick and span as when you do it. And how do you make them smell so beautiful? *Aha!*" Triumphantly, she waved a pair of shorts and a sleeveless tunic—made from the most delicate of petals—in the air, before diving back beneath the plant again.

"The secret is in my special soap," said Lavender brightly. She scooped up the purple petals and admired them. "And a sprinkling of fairy magic, of course," she added quietly to herself.

Candytuft's leaves trembled alarmingly as the little fairy searched among the stems. At last, she found what she was looking for.

"Ta-daaa!" she announced, bringing out a small pile of white petals. "Handkerchiefs!" she explained. "Ooops—here are more!"

She spied another heap of white petals lying beside her cooking pot and gave everything to Lavender. "That's everything!" she said cheerfully.

"Now, are you *really* sure you don't mind?"

"Not at all," said Lavender, looking genuinely delighted at the prospect of sinking her arms into a tub of soapy suds. "That's what friends are for." And she fluttered away in the direction of the stream.

Candytuft waved goodbye, then rubbed her hands together delightedly. Now it was her turn. And although she might be terrible at laundry, she was an absolute whiz at making sweets. And luckily, she'd made huge batches of her two most popular treats just the week before. She had more than enough Snapdragon Sherberts and Marigold Mallows to treat the whole of Flower Fairyland.

"Excellent," said Candytuft briskly to herself. Perhaps she could wrap the sweets with her leaves and decorate each package with a tiny flower . . . That really would look lovely. She thought of her friends' faces when she presented them with her gifts—they were sure to be thrilled.

"Now, where are those sweets?" muttered Candytuft, whose other great talent was talking. She was so chatty that she'd talk to anyone and everyone about anything and everything. The weather . . . the latest fairy fashions . . . which shoots were peeping through the soil . . . who the handsome Kingcup might dance with at the Midsummer Party . . . She would talk to whoever would listen, whether they were a Flower Fairy, a bird or a bee. And if there wasn't a soul nearby, then Candytuft would simply talk to herself. She was a very good audience.

The pretty fairy hopped lightly about the flower bed where her plant grew, using her gossamer wings to lift her a little higher. Like the other Garden Flower Fairies, Candytuft didn't fly long distances. She walked, skipped or hopped as much as she could, tending only to take to the air when she wanted to reach a tree, or even just for fun. If she had to travel further afield, she

would hitch a lift with an obliging bird or a dragonfly.

"I'm sure I left them here," Candytuft told a passing wasp.

It buzzed helpfully in reply, nosing gently around the clusters of pretty pink, white and

purple blossoms.

"Oh no . . ." said Candytuft. It all came flooding back. Last weekend, she'd happily handed over her entire sweet supplies to the Midsummer Party committee. Every last treat. So she had nothing to give her fairy

friends this week. "What shall I do?" she
cried.

The wasp buzzed in her ear. And then it
buzzed away.

Candytuft sighed and shook her head.
The wasp was right. There was only one
solution—and that was to make more sweets
for her friends. It would mean quite a lot
of hard work, but if she stirred and mixed
like crazy, she might have just enough time

to create some wonderful treats for Fairy Friendship Week.

It was not in Candytuft's nature to be worried for long and her mind was soon brimming with wonderful ideas. She would make Lavender a batch of mouth-watering Lavender Creams, Periwinkle was sure to appreciate a selection of Periwinkle Puffs and everyone loved Fairy Fudge. In case anyone was thirsty, she would fill hazel-nut shells with her famous Dandelion and

Burdock Juice, created in honor of her two dearest friends. The juice was quite tricky to make—once, Candytuft had stirred in the wrong direction while whispering a

charm and the sparkling drink had turned to sludge—so she intended to follow the recipe to the letter.

She stood on tiptoes to reach her petal apron, which was slung over a nearby stem, and glanced around for her beloved recipe book. Not being the tidiest fairy in the Flower Fairies' Garden, Candytuft wasn't worried when she didn't spot it immediately. She looked in all the usual places—beside the cooking pot, in between her spoons and inside her storage shells—but the recipe book was nowhere to be seen. So she looked in all the unusual places too. But there was still no sign of the tattered old recipe book,

whose white petal pages curled at the edges
and whose words were smudged where she'd
accidentally dropped mixture on to them.

And suddenly, Candytuft remembered.
She *had* left her recipe book in one of the
usual places. It had lain beside her cooking
pot, looking—if a fairy were to glance very
quickly and not pay too much attention—
just like a small heap of white petal
handkerchiefs.

"Oh, no," groaned Candytuft. Her shoulders, her wings and even her blonde curls sagged disconsolately.

Her precious book of magical recipes was in the wash.

There wasn't a moment to lose. "Stop!" cried Candytuft, as she sped through the garden, leaving a trail of surprised Flower Fairies in her wake. "Stop! Fire! No, not fire, sorry ... But stop! *Please*!"

"What on earth is the matter?" asked a very worried Lavender, when Candytuft skidded to a halt beside the stream, almost overbalancing into the water.

"*Please* tell me that you haven't washed my handkerchiefs yet," pleaded Candytuft, her sweet little face flushed bright pink after her cross-garden dash.

Wordlessly, Lavender lifted sodden, white petals from the stream.

Chapter Two
Try and Try Again

Candytuft stared at the spotlessly clean recipe book. The blank white petals seemed to mock her with their emptiness. She sighed forlornly. All of her valuable recipes had vanished—not a single word or a letter remained.

Lavender had been absolutely mortified when she'd discovered what had happened, but Candytuft smiled bravely and tried to look as if it wasn't too much of a problem. "It was my silly fault," she said, with a forced laugh. "It's about

time that I invented some new treats anyway!"

But in the privacy of her own plant, her greatest fear bubbled to the surface. "What if I can never make delicious sweets again?" she

said to herself as a single shiny tear ran down her cheek.

The wasp flew past, pausing to buzz in Candytuft's ear and, for the first time since she'd discovered her mistake, the little

Flower Fairy smiled. "You're absolutely right, of course," she told the friendly insect. "I can't let one itsy-bitsy problem like a total lack of recipes spoil things." She squared her shoulders determinedly. "I'll experiment!"

The very first step was to hunt for ingredients. Candytuft put a large sack woven from dried stems over one shoulder

and marched purposefully around the Flower Fairies' Garden. And, once she explained her situation to the fairies she met, they fell over themselves to provide her with as many goodies as she could carry.

Crab-apple gave her two fine fruits that she'd stored during the long winter. "They're a little bit sour," she warned. "I like them that way, but you might want to add a smidgen of honey to sweeten them up a little."

"That's a great idea," Candytuft said, carefully tucking the crab apples inside

her sack. "Thank you so much."

The round, cuddly fairy who lived in the mulberry bush was reaching into a handful of plump berries when Candytuft passed by.

"Oh, there you are!" he called, the perky
stem on his dark red cap waving to and fro.
"I heard that you needed some tasty morsels
and I've collected you a *huge* pile of berries!"
He wiped a dribble of berry juice from his
chin and cleared his throat guiltily. "That
is . . . it *was* a huge pile."

Candytuft stifled a giggle. She knew how
much the little fairy loved to eat, and also
that he regularly shared his purple-red fruit

with the hungry silkworms
that lived on his branches.
"If you can spare them,"
she said, "I'd love to take a
couple of clusters."

"Is that all?" said Mulberry,
relief lighting up his face. "Here
you go!" And he tossed two bunches
of closely packed fruit down to her.
Candytuft couldn't believe how kind
everyone was. She collected bundles of sweet

stamens, slivers of silvery bark and heaps of petals. The generous bees gave her a whole, sticky honeycomb too. Her sack was soon bulging. It was extremely heavy too—so heavy that she had to sprinkle a pinch of precious fairy dust on to it to make it lighter for the journey home.

Back at her flower, Candytuft donned her pink-and-white striped petal apron and set to work. Her cooking pot was a sturdy old horse-chestnut case that she'd toughened with fairy magic. It was perfect for cooking because, when it was upended, the spikes poked into the ground so that it didn't wobble. She rubbed the inside with a lime leaf to make sure it was perfectly clean and to add a lovely tangy flavor to the sweets.

"And now for my first ingredient!" announced Candytuft, bowing to her small but appreciative audience—Dandelion and Burdock. She broke off seven tiny mulberries and dropped them into the pot.

"Now for my *second* ingredient!" she said, and added a splash of morning dew. "And my third . . ." Essence of plum—a whole handful—tumbled into the pot. She went to dip an acorn cup into the mixture and then swiftly changed her mind.

"What are you doing, Candytuft?" asked Dandelion curiously. He swung on a nearby branch, his dazzling yellow and green outfit and beautiful wings glowing as brightly as the sun.

She paused, her foot in mid-air. "Why, I'm getting in, of course." She grinned broadly at Dandelion's horrified expression and hopped into the cooking pot. "I won't extract the full, delicious flavor of the mulberries simply by stirring," she explained. She stepped lightly from side to side, feeling the tiny berries

squish and pop
beneath her toes.

"Oh my," said
Burdock, his
eyebrows arching so
high that they looked in
danger of floating up, up and
away from his forehead. "You did wash
your feet, didn't you . . . ?"

Precisely 101 steps later—which was
when Candytuft felt that
the mixture was just
right—she prepared
some magic words,
wishing desperately
that she could have

remembered the old ones in her recipe book.
She scattered a pinch of fairy dust on to
the purple-red surface of the mixture and
whispered the new charm . . . *"Softer than cloud,
luscious and light, sweets to lift spirits to a dizzying
height."*

Instantly, the mulberry potion thickened,
gaining a glossy shine. Candytuft smiled.
This was going much better than she'd
hoped. Happily, she plunged her hands into

the horse-chestnut case and began to roll
the mixture into a variety of shapes, laying
these gently on to a green leaf to dry. "I
shall call these... Mulberry Nuggets!" she
announced.

"Bravo!" shouted Dandelion and Burdock.
"Can we try them?"

Beaming with pride, Candytuft offered
them the leafy tray of sticky sweets and
drifted off into a wonderful daydream

where Flower Fairies were crowding round to congratulate her on the new sweets. She hadn't lost her touch, after all. She could still make the best treats in all Flower Fairyland!

"Ew!" said Dandelion, looking rather horrified.

Burdock turned a pale shade of green that was remarkably similar to his leggings. "I don't think they're your greatest creation…"

he said politely, and hiccupped.

But worse was to come. Candytuft watched in horror as, without a single flap of their wings, Dandelion and Burdock rose above the ground before sailing right up into the air. Too surprised to cry out, their mouths formed Os of astonishment.

"Oh my goodness!" cried Candytuft. Her charm had gone terribly wrong. Somehow, instead of lifting the fairies'

spirits to dizzying heights, she'd lifted the Flower Fairies themselves!

She switched immediately into auto-fairy mode and reached for the emergency pinch of fairy dust that was safely hidden in her waistband. *"Fairy dust, fairy dust, back down to earth!"* she cried, flinging the magic sparkles upwards.

She held her breath anxiously. Would this charm work . . . or would her best friends be trapped high in the treetops forever?

Chapter Three
Meddlesome Mischief

Fortunately, the power of the Mulberry Nuggets was no match for Candytuft's counter spell, and Dandelion and Burdock floated gently back down to earth. They were very matter-of-fact about the whole adventure and bravely offered to test more of Candytuft's experimental sweets.

"It's really rather exciting," said Dandelion, who was always up for new experiences. His twinkling eyes showed that he wasn't in the slightest bit angry.

"But no mulberries," insisted Burdock with a shudder. "Something sweeter

next time, please. And not quite so uplifting."

"Oh, of course!" insisted Candytuft, relieved beyond belief that her tasters hadn't deserted her. "I'm sure it won't happen again, you know."

But it did.

The Hazelnut Nougat made Burdock's brown wings turn bright orange—they smelt of orange too, which was very strange. And when Dandelion tried the Silver-Birch Brittle he began to bark like a dog. As for the Fuschia Fondants . . . well, the two Flower Fairies weren't wild about their fingernails turning bright pink. As soon as they could, they made up an excuse and left, to be replaced by more eager fairy volunteers. By now, news of Candytuft's exploits had travelled far and wide.

But there were sweet successes too. With tiny alterations to her recipe for Mulberry

Nuggets, Candytuft created delightful sweets that melted on the tongue without sending Flower Fairies shooting up into the trees. Her Crab-Apple Chunks—apple pieces coated with a sweet honey crust—were declared to be irresistible by everyone who tasted them, and the first batch only made the fairies' ears grow a *tiny* bit pointier . . .

Before long, Candytuft had stopped fretting and started enjoying herself instead.

She began to realize that she'd been so used to making the same sweets from her trusty recipe book over and over again that she'd forgotten what fun it was to create something totally new.

"I'm never going to get stuck in a rut again," she told Celandine fairy, who'd

dropped by to sample the latest offerings. "Classic, traditional sweets are all very well, but everyone likes a change, don't they?

Although . . ." she added, gazing into her cooking pot wistfully, "I do so wish I could rediscover the recipe for Fairy Fudge—"

"C-c-candytuft," interrupted Celandine.

Candytuft dipped a finger into the latest mixture—Daisy Chews—and thoughtfully slurped it clean. "Mmm . . ." she said, distracted by the delicious taste. "Yes?" she asked.

There was no reply and Candytuft looked up to see that Celandine was quietly sobbing into a yellow petal handkerchief. "Whatever's the matter?" she gasped. "Oh, I'm so sorry! Here I am, chattering away about myself and I didn't ask how you are . . . Do tell me what's wrong. I'll listen, I really will."

Celandine pushed her beautiful auburn hair away from her face. She sniffed a little and clenched her dainty hands into fists, screwing the handkerchief into a ball as she did so. For a moment, she looked so agitated that Candytuft wasn't even sure she'd be able to speak. But then the words started tumbling out, like water from an underground spring.

"I shouldn't s-s-say," she stammered. "It's just that it's s-s-so upsetting."

"Oh, poor Celandine!' said Candytuft, flinging a slightly sticky arm around her shoulders. "Tell me everything." She led the trembling Flower Fairy to a mossy cushion. Obediently, Celandine sat down, folding her glorious greeny-yellow wings and spreading the long yellow petals of her skirt carefully

around her, while she calmed down. Then, whispering in a voice so quiet that Candytuft had to lean close to hear, she began to speak.

It was a sorry tale indeed. As part of Fairy Friendship Week, Celandine had decided to make some new slippers for Dandelion—his were looking shabby and worn. Rather than bothering him for materials, and to make it even more of a surprise, she'd used her own tough leaves, snipping and shaping the green slippers until they were just right. Now, all she'd needed was a dandelion seed head to make a fluffy pompom for each slipper. For this, she *had* to visit Dandelion—there was no part of her flower that would do.

"S-s-so I went to find him," said Celandine. "But h-h-he was nowhere to be found."

This was no great surprise to Candytuft. She knew how much Dandelion liked to travel. After all, his flower would grow anywhere, so why would he want to live in one place?

"And when I got home—" here, Celandine gave a great, heaving sob—"the slippers were r-r-ruined, torn to shreds!"

"Do you have any idea what happened?" asked Candytuft gently. She was sure there had to be some rational explanation. This sort of thing just didn't happen in Flower Fairyland.

"It was D-d-dandelion. He did it!" Celandine burst into tears once again.

For once in her life, Candytuft was speechless with shock and disbelief. Then her chatty tongue wiggled into action once more. "But how do you know?" she asked. "Why would Dandelion ruin a present that you'd made for him?" Dandelion was one of Candytuft's best

friends. He wouldn't do such a thing, would he . . . ?

"W-w-when I got back, I found dandelion petals scattered everywhere," Celandine said, her chocolate-brown eyes filled with sadness. "It's the truth," she said. "I can't imagine why he did it, but he *did*, Candytuft. He did."

"We must ask him what happened," said Candytuft firmly. She was a great believer in hearing both sides of a story.

But Celandine vetoed the suggestion at once. "We *can't*!" she cried, utterly horrified by the suggestion. "It's Fairy Friendship Week. We can't accuse another fairy of unneighborly behavior at the friendliest time of the year!"

Chapter Four
More Strange Happenings

Reluctantly, Candytuft agreed that they should let sleeping fairies lie. After she'd dried her tears, Celandine insisted that she wasn't upset anymore—Candytuft didn't believe a word of it—and that she would simply make another pair of slippers for Dandelion. So, furnished with a bundle of freshly made and exceedingly sticky treats, she made her way home.

Thoroughly bemused, Candytuft went back to her cooking pot, where she tried to make sense of it all. "It's just not Dandelion's style," she muttered to herself, adding a smidgen of corn and some yellow stamens to the mixture. "He's kind and he's thoughtful. He helps other fairies, he doesn't upset them."

Fairy footsteps approached. "Talking to yourself again?" asked Burdock, dragging a handful of brown stems laden with bristly burrs. "You need to get out more!" he chortled.

"Not much chance of that, this week," said Candytuft, grimacing. She took the solid lump of candy from her cooking pot and plonked it on to a clean leaf, before rolling it out with a smooth, thick stem. "Well, what do you know, Burdock?" she asked, certain that her friend would entertain her. "Come on ... spill the beans. While I'm stuck here, it's up to you to bring the news to *me*."

"Hmm . . . I'm not sure I should say."
Burdock's usually sunny expression darkened.
"But I have to tell someone." He crouched
down beside Candytuft, who had stopped
rolling as soon as she'd heard his tone.
"My news isn't good," he went on. "In fact,
it's downright dreadful."

"What's the matter?" she asked, feeling distinctly uneasy.

So Burdock explained. As a favor to the other fairies during Fairy Friendship Week, he had decided to provide a complimentary spring-cleaning service. Armed with his trusty burr brush, he had patrolled the garden in search of messy places in need of a good cleaning. And, while each lucky Flower Fairy was away from his or her flower, he'd taken the opportunity to sweep and prune and tidy to his heart's content.

"But what's dreadful about that?" asked Candytuft.

Burdock sighed. "When I'd finished, I revisited each flower, just to admire their loveliness," he said. "But each and every one was as messy as can be. If anything, they were *worse* than before I'd started! And now I just don't know why I bothered. The fairies don't appreciate my friendly behavior at all." He hung his head and absent-mindedly fiddled with the tassels on his burgundy tunic. "There's more," he said reluctantly. "I found evidence—the culprits dropped their own petals everywhere."

"But who—?"

Burdock shook his head. "I won't say who it is," he said stubbornly.

Candytuft patted her dear friend's shoulder and frowned. Strange things were afoot in the Flower Fairies' Garden, and no mistake. "We should ask around to find out what's going on," she said.

But Burdock was just as reluctant as Celandine to discuss the matter with the rest of the fairies. "What if I'm wrong?" he demanded, gabbling at great speed. "There could be other explanations. What if I got the flowers mixed up? What if a small but very

fierce tornado whipped through the garden when my back was turned?"

"How about you take a break?" said Candytuft in her most calming voice. She

hastily pressed a few flower shapes from the rolled-flat mixture and gave them to Burdock. "You've had a nasty shock," she said. "Take these Daisy Chews back home and try to relax a little. Let me deal with this."

Burdock nodded and, looking very relieved, scurried away.

Candytuft pondered the facts for a long,

long time, but she came no closer to solving the mysteries that Burdock and Celandine had confided in her. All she knew was that the harmony of Fairy Friendship Week was at stake. And if she didn't do something about it, the peace and friendliness that made the Flower Fairies' Garden such a wonderful place to live would be gone forever.

Chapter Five
Mysterious Visitors

For a fairy who was used to roaming around in search of conversation, Candytuft found it hard to believe that she could hear so much gossip by staying in one place. There was no need to go looking for clues. Once they realized that she was confined to her open-air kitchen, the other fairies visited regularly. And they came laden with more strange tales.

Candytuft discovered that Celandine and Burdock weren't the only fairies to suffer bad luck. The petals from one of Rose's most magnificent blooms had been scattered around her rose garden—and she'd found one of

Zinnia's unmistakable pink petals amid the disorder. Then someone stole all the fluffy seeds from Dandelion's clocks, so he couldn't tell the time. Dandelion told Candytuft that he'd found one of Celandine's long yellow petals wrapped around a stem and tied in a big, floppy bow.

More and more fairies came to see Candytuft with their tales of woe—all of them highly confidential. Everyone was talking to her about the strange goings on, but no one was talking to each other. Before long, Candytuft knew so many secrets that she barely opened her mouth for fear of blurting any of them out. Instead, she took careful notes. The evidence was sure to come in very handy.

"If only I had enough sweets to go round," she muttered to her cooking pot when there was no one within earshot—she could only imagine that there was a lull in the mischief. "Then I could stop making sweets and start making enquiries instead." She turned round to check her stockpile of sweets and got the biggest shock of her life. The great heap of fairy treats stretched so high into the air that it reached past the top of her flower. "My goodness," she said. "I *have* been busy . . ."

She had more than enough sweets to treat the whole Flower Fairies' Garden twice—maybe three times—over!

Candytuft beamed with delight and then peered into her cooking pot, which contained a kaleidoscope of pale pink, vivid purple and snowy white. She was preparing Candytuft Fudge—a brand-new concoction of utter deliciousness made from her very own petals and a few very secret ingredients that she'd collected on her expedition around the garden.

"Ahem," said a gruff voice.

Candytuft spun round to face some of the most awkward-looking fairies she'd ever laid eyes on. There were three of them—a small fairy flanked by two much heftier companions. All wore curious outfits made up of emerald, ivy and lime green leaves, sewn together in a higgledy-piggledy fashion. And tied on each of their heads was a large petal bonnet made from a mishmash of dandelion, rose, celandine and zinnia petals, with a burdock burr perched on top. The bonnets hung low over their brows and entirely covered their ears, but not their glittery dark eyes or their pointed noses.

The smallest fairy cleared his throat again. "It's Fairy Friendship Week," he said. "We want to eat your sweets. Give us some." One of the bigger fairies nudged him. "Please," he muttered.

Candytuft had never known a fairy to act in this way and she was quite taken aback. But she tried not to let it show and gave a tinkling laugh instead. "But of course," she said, stirring briskly. "Although . . . we fairies usually give presents because we *want* to, rather than being asked for them."

"Sweets," growled the little fairy. "Now."

"I haven't seen you around these parts,"

said Candytuft, biding her time. She wanted to be quite sure of her facts before she pounced. "Have you come far?"

"Yes—" said one of the bigger fairies, but a stern look from the fairy-in-charge silenced him. "Er . . . no."

"We live here," insisted the leader. "We are the fairies. Now, where are those sweets? We like sweets."

By now, Candytuft's senses were on red alert. She decided to go for it. "You like causing mischief too, don't you?" She stopped stirring, placed her hands firmly on her hips and conjured up her angriest glare, which she directed right at the visitors.

They spluttered with indignation, huffing and puffing like old-fashioned steam trains. "We never . . . how dare . . . mischief?" The smallest fairy was quite beside himself.

"Then how do you explain these?" asked Candytuft, pointing to the collection of petals decorating his bonnet. "Which fairy *are* you, exactly? Where are *your* petals? You seem to be wearing a whole bunch of petals that I know for a fact belong to other Flower Fairies."

At once, all their bravado leaked away. The three suspects hung their heads guiltily. They knew they'd been found out.

"And I suppose you could tell me a thing or two about the mischief that's been going on," said Candytuft. She leant forward and plucked the smallest fairy's bonnet from his head. "Couldn't you, Mr Elf?"

The game was up. On his head was a pair

of exceedingly pointy and very long elf ears.
These were no Flower Fairies—these were
elves!

Chapter Six
Sweet Victory

"Mischief is what we like doing best," explained the smallest elf.

It was much later and the three elves were slurping elderflower tea from hazelnut shells. Much to Candytuft's surprise, she'd found it was very easy to forgive the naughty elves, who kept making her laugh with their odd comments. But all the same, she was determined that they should put things right.

"You've made a lot of fairies very sad indeed," she said seriously. "Your naughtiness has threatened some of the strongest friendships in Flower Fairyland. Playing tricks is bad enough, but leaving fake clues so the Flower Fairies would blame each other is shocking behavior. You'll have to make amends." She dealt the final blow. "You'll have to apologize."

"Oh no," said the smallest elf quite insistently. "We're really not very good at saying sorry. We're much better at causing mayhem. We're the elves, you know."

"That's a shame," said Candytuft, daintily sipping her tea. "And I was going to give you some sweets to take home with you too. Ah, well . . . never mind."

"Er . . . sweets, you say?" the elf laughed nervously. "Well, I suppose we could come to some arrangement—in the interests of fairy friendship, you understand. Not because we've gone soft."

"Of course not," said Candytuft, quickly turning to her cooking pot to hide her smiles. "Just let me put the finishing touches to my Candytuft Fudge..."

The most brilliant idea had popped into her head—an idea so cunning that the elves themselves would have been proud of it. She would lace the candy mixture with an honesty enchantment. When the elves ate the sweets they would feel compelled to be totally truthful.

"Fairy dust, fairy dust, please tell the truth," she whispered, as she sprinkled a generous pinch of fairy dust into the sweet concoction, quickly stirring it in to hide the telltale sparkles. "And that's the whole truth, and nothing but the truth," she added, to be on the safe side.

In less time than it takes a Flower Fairy to flutter their wings, the Candytuft Fudge was ready. And it looked wonderful. Its pink, purple and white marbling swirled through the fudge like a wobbly rainbow. It was shiny and sticky. It was irresistible. It was *perfect*.

"Well, we'd best be off then," said the elves, tripping over their pointy shoes in their eagerness to get their hands on

the fudge.

"Please try some before you go," said Candytuft sweetly. "And be sure to visit these fairies first." She gave them a pink petal inscribed with fairy names: Celandine, Burdock, Dandelion, Rose and Zinnia. The elves nodded. "Mmm ... mm-mm ... *mmm* ... mmm," they said, their mouths far too full of sticky fudge for them to speak properly. They heaved sacks of sweets on to their shoulders and waved goodbye.

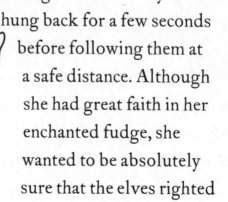

"And don't forget to clean your teeth this evening!" called Candytuft. She hung back for a few seconds before following them at a safe distance. Although she had great faith in her enchanted fudge, she wanted to be absolutely sure that the elves righted their wrongs. Fairy friendship was far too important to leave to chance.

Giggling merrily to themselves, the elves scampered through the garden, so happy that they leapt into the air and tapped their heels together in delight. They reached Celandine's flower first, nestled by the side of a sunny footpath.

"Yoohoo!" called one of the elves, "We've come to tell you the truth!" He froze, horrified by his own words. "What I mean to say," he corrected himself, "is that we've come to ap—" The little elf clamped his lips shut before he could say the dreaded word. But it slipped out anyway. "Apologize!"

"What's that?" said Celandine. She appeared from behind her flower. In her hands were a pair of half-finished green slippers and a needle and thread.

"He said that we've come to apologize,"

repeated one of the bigger elves. He shrugged helplessly as the last elf threw him a cross look. "Can't help it, boss," he said. "I know you don't want to tell this lovely fairy that we ruined Dandelion's slippers, but—"

"Shush!" hissed the other elf. "You'll be telling her that we planted fake evidence next!"

"Ooops," said the third elf. "Sorry, Celandine," he said gruffly to the astonished Flower Fairy. "Want some sweets?" Candytuft hugged herself gleefully. Even from this distance—she was safely hidden behind the lavender bush—she could see that Celandine was thrilled by the revelations.

A gentle smile brightened her glum face. "So it wasn't Dandelion?" Celandine said, as the truth slowly sank in. "It was you all along." She tried to look stern, but was much too nice a fairy to be angry for long. "Well, I think that's very brave of you to tell the truth." She grasped the smallest elf's hand firmly and pumped it up and down. Then she looked at the sweets they'd brought. "And you're delivering Candytuft's gifts too. Well, isn't that the kindest thing."

The elves had the decency to look embarrassed, but seemed to enjoy being on the receiving end of compliments for a change and smiled broadly. "Well, we must dash," said the little elf. "No rest for the wicked." He checked the list and sauntered off in the direction of Burdock's home, his companions following on behind.

Candytuft smiled contentedly as she listened to the astonished cries and cheery laughter that was soon echoing all around as the elves unwittingly revealed all to everyone they met. To think that the Flower Fairies' Garden might by now be riddled with suspicion and lies if she hadn't mixed up her washing! And with that thought Candytuft skipped into the garden to join her fairy friends.

FLOWER FAIRIES™ FRIENDS

Visit our Flower Fairies website at:

www.flowerfairies.com

There are lots of fun Flower Fairy games and activities for you to play, plus you can find out more about all your favorite fairy friends!

Log onto the
Flower Fairies
Friendship Ring

Visit the Flower Fairies website to sign up for the new Flower Fairies Friendship Ring!

★ No membership fee

★ Newsletter updates

★ Every new friend receives a special gift!
(while supplies last)